JAMES MAYHEW studied illustration at Maidstone College of Art.
In 1994 he won one of the New York Times Ten Best Illustrated Books awards
for his work on *The Boy and the Cloth of Dreams*. He is perhaps best known
for the Katie books introducing children to art, which he wrote and illustrated.
Recently he has been writing stories for other illustrators,
including Caroline Jayne Church and Lindsey Gardiner.

JACKIE MORRIS's highly acclaimed illustrated books include
Ted Hughes' *How the Whale Became*, Sian Lewis' *Cities in the Sea*,
winner of the Tir Na N-Og Award 1997, Susan Summers' *The Greatest Gift*
and Sydney Carter's *Lord of the Dance*. Her Frances Lincoln books
include collaborations with Caroline Pitcher on *The Snow Whale*,
The Time of the Lion, Mariana and the Merchild and *Lord of the Forest*,
and with Mary Hoffman on *Parables, Miracles* and *Animals of the Bible*.
Recently she wrote and illustrated *The Seal Children*,
winner of the Tir Na N-Og Award 2005.

For Evie, who is a little wild thing,
and for Buddy and all his friends
at Keinton Mandeville school – Jackie M.

For Tom and Hannah

and their brilliant Mum, Jackie – James M.

First published in Great Britain and the USA in 2005 by Frances Lincoln Children's Books,
4 Torriano Mews, Torriano Avenue, London NW5 2RZ
www.franceslincoln.com

First paperback edition published in Great Britain and the USA in 2006

A catalogue record for this book is available from the British Library.

Frances Lincoln edition
ISBN 13: 978-1-84507-364-0

Printed in Dongguan, Guangdong China by Toppan Leefung in February 2012
3 5 7 9 8 6 4

Visit the Jackie Morris website at
www.jackiemorris.co.uk

Can You See A Little Bear?

Written by James Mayhew
Illustrated by Jackie Morris

F

FRANCES LINCOLN
CHILDREN'S BOOKS

Elephants are big,

mice are small,

Can you see **a little bear**

standing on **a ball?**

Lions are yellow, peacocks are blue,

Can you see a little bear trying on a shoe?

Snakes are thin,
a walrus is fat,

Can you see a little bear trying on a hat?

Parrots can be **green**

and parrots can be **red**,

Can you see **a little bear** standing on **his head?**

Giraffes are tall,

guinea-pigs are short,

Can you see **the toy** that **a little bear** has bought?

Whales can swim and seagulls fly,

Can you see **a little bear** flying very high?

Ducks like the rain,

penguins like the snow,

Here's Little Bear –
and he's putting on a show!

Chickens like the **day**,

foxes like

the night,

Can you see a big bear

carrying a light?

Camels like the **desert**,

dolphins like the **sea**,

Can you see **a little bear**

going home for **tea**?

Crocodiles **cry**
and kookaburras **laugh**,

Now it's time for **Little Bear** to have a little **bath!**

Deer can **run**...

and hares can **leap**...

I think **Little Bear** is almost fast asleep.

Cats like the sun
and owls like the moon,

Good night, Little Bear –
hope to see you soon!

OTHER JACKIE MORRIS TITLES
FROM FRANCES LINCOLN CHILDREN'S BOOKS

THE SEAL CHILDREN
Jackie Morris

For the people of a remote Welsh village, emigrating to a more
prosperous life in the New World is no more than a distant dream.
But one day Ffion and Morlo, the children of Huw and his selkie wife,
recall their mother singing of cities beneath the waves,
shining cities of gold and pearls…

LORD OF THE FOREST
Caroline Pitcher
Illustrated by Jackie Morris

For little Tiger, each new sound he hears in the forest is exciting.
But every time he tells his mother, she replies, "When you don't hear them,
my son, be ready. The Lord of the Forest is here!" Tiger is puzzled,
and as he grows bigger, he asks all his friends – strutting Peacock,
blundering Rhino and trumpeting Elephant – to help him decide
who is the Lord of the Forest?

THE TIME OF THE LION
Caroline Pitcher
Illustrated by Jackie Morris

At night-time, when Joseph hears a Lion's roar, he decides, against
his father's advice, to go and meet the Lion. He sleeps beside him,
meets his brave lioness and watches the cubs play,
learning that danger is not always where you think.
Then one day traders come looking for lion cubs …

Frances Lincoln titles are available from all good bookshops.
You can also buy books and find out more about your favourite titles,
authors and illustrators at our website: www.franceslincoln.com